ANDROCLES AND THE LION

Retold by Catherine Storr
Illustrated by Philip Hood

Methuen Children's Books
in association with Belitha Press Ltd.

Note: The story of Androcles is very old. Aesop wrote a version of it, and Aulus Gellius included it in his *Gesta Romanorum*. The most famous modern version is the play *Androcles and the Lion* by George Bernard Shaw, which he intended for children – but it is rarely performed with children in mind!

C.S.

Copyright © in this format Belitha Press Ltd, 1986
Text copyright © Catherine Storr 1986
Illustrations copyright © Philip Hood 1986
Art Director: Treld Bicknell
First published in Great Britain in 1986
by Methuen Children's Books Ltd,
11 New Fetter Lane, London EC4P 4EE
Conceived, designed and produced by Belitha Press Ltd,
31 Newington Green, London N16 9PU
ISBN 0 416 96110 X (hardback)
ISBN 0 416 96120 7 (paperback)
Printed in Hong Kong by South China Printing Co.

NEARLY TWO THOUSAND YEARS AGO, IN NORTHERN AFRICA,
there lived a poor slave called Androcles.
His master was a rich Roman citizen,
who treated his slaves with great cruelty.
Often Androcles was beaten so badly
that he could hardly crawl home to his hut,
where he lived with his wife, Numia, and his little son.
"If I hadn't got you, I would run away,"
he often said to Numia.
"If you ran away, what would become of us?
The master would punish us for your disobedience.
And you know that if you were caught,
the punishment is death," Numia said.

"The master's wife, our mistress, hates me.
Yesterday the master had told me to move the big mother pig
and her twelve little piglets to a new feeding place,
further from his house. When I had done it,
and caught all those frisky little piglets,
the mistress came out and said they should not have been moved at all.
She made her husband beat me," Androcles said.
"Wait till our son is older.
Then perhaps we could all escape together," Numia said.
"But I don't know where we could go to.
The country beyond here is all mountains and forests,
full of wild animals.
If we escaped the Roman soldiers,
we should probably be killed and eaten
by the lions or the panthers in the forests."

ONE DAY A VERY GRAND ROMAN CITIZEN, A SENATOR,
came to stay with Androcles's master.
He happened to see Numia working in the house
and he asked who she was.
"Sell her to me to take back to Rome
as a present for the Emperor."
Numia's master was delighted to be offered so much money,
and he agreed.

Numia wept. "Don't separate me from my husband!
Let me stay here,
and I will work harder than ever for you," she pleaded.
But her master would not listen. Then Numia said,
"At least do not separate me from my little son.
If you take me and leave him behind, I shall kill myself."
Her master was afraid that if she kept her word,
he would be forced to return the money
that was to be paid for her,
so he agreed that she might take her son with her.

WHEN ANDROCLES CAME BACK TO HIS HUT THAT NIGHT,
he found it empty and cold.
His neighbours told him
how Numia had been carried away with the child
and that she had been sold as a slave for the Emperor.
Androcles knew that it would be useless
to try to plead with his master.
"But I cannot stay here without Numia and my son.
I shall run away.
Perhaps I shall be lucky and find a way of reaching Rome,
where I might see them again," he thought.

That night he stole out of his master's grounds
and went out into the wild country.
He was frightened of the dark,
he did not know where to go,
he knew that if he was overtaken by the soldiers
he would be put to death,
and he was terrified of the wild beasts.
But anything was better than staying with his cruel master,
now that his wife and child were gone.

For TWO DAYS, ANDROCLES WALKED ACROSS MOORS
and scrubby bushland,
towards the mountains he could see in the distance.
He fed on berries and roots,
and whenever he saw any people, he hid,
for fear of being caught by the Roman soldiers.
At last he reached the foothills of the mountains,
so hungry and so tired that he could go no further.
He saw the opening of a cave in the side of the nearest hill.
"I will hide in there for the rest of the day," he thought.
"If I am alive tomorrow morning
I may be able to go on further."
He threw himself on the floor of the cave and slept.

HE WAS WOKEN BY A SOUND
which filled him with terror.
He started up,
and saw a huge shape
at the entrance of the cave.

A lion was coming towards him,
roaring as it came. "This is the end.
Now I am about to be killed and eaten,"
Androcles thought.

But the lion did not fall upon him as he expected.
Instead it stood a little way off,
holding up one of its paws,
and Androcles realised that the sound it was making
was not the savage roar of a hungry beast,
but the cry of an animal in pain.

He dared to crawl a little nearer,
and now he saw that the paw was swollen and bloody
and there was a large thorn sticking out of the soft flesh
behind the talons.
Androcles was frightened, but he had a kind heart.
"You poor beast! If you would let me,
I could take that thorn out of your paw
and make you much more comfortable," he said.

The lion was perhaps soothed by his kind voice,
for it did not move as Androcles dared to go right up to it
and take the wounded paw in his hand.
"Don't eat me up yet," he said to the lion.
"Wait a minute or two till I've finished this little job."
And very gently, he eased the huge thorn out of the lion's paw.
The lion licked its paw clean.
Then, to Androcles' surprise,
it lay down on the floor of the cave and went to sleep.
"Tomorrow it will eat me," Androcles thought,
and he too lay down and slept.

THE NEXT DAY, THE LION'S PAW WAS NOT SO SWOLLEN,
and though it was still lame, it left the cave in the morning
without trying to eat Androcles.
In the evening he saw it come limping back
with food in its mouth, which it laid at Androcles's feet.
Androcles was very hungry.

"May I share your supper, King of the beasts?" he asked.
He stretched out his hand to the food,
and the lion did not try to stop him.
Then Androcles knew that the animal was grateful
to him for curing the wounded paw
and that it looked on him as a friend.

FOR A LONG TIME, THE MAN AND THE BEAST SHARED THE CAVE.
No soldiers came into the mountains to search for a runaway slave.
Androcles began to feel safe.
But he missed the company of other men
and especially he missed his wife and his little son.
At first he had been careful when he left the cave,
and never went near roads or villages where he might be seen.
But as time went on, he grew careless,
and one day a group of villagers saw him
and reported him to the Governor of the province,
who sent a band of soldiers to capture him.

"SIR, WE FOUND THIS MAN IN THE MOUNTAINS,
but he will not tell us how he came to be there,"
the captain of the soldiers said.
The Governor asked Androcles:
"How did you come to be living in the wild?
You cannot be a freeman.
Confess now, you are a slave who has broken his bond
and run away from his kind master."
When Androcles did not answer this,
the Governor said to the soldiers,
"Get out the whips and beat this man
until he finds his tongue."
Androcles fell on his knees. "Sir, do not have me beaten.
It is true, I was a slave.
But my master was not kind.
He treated me cruelly and he sold my wife
to a Roman who has taken her to give to the Emperor.
After that my life was so miserable that I ran away."
"Nonsense!" replied the Governor,
"You ran away because you were stupid and ungrateful,
and you have done yourself no good.
You deserve the punishment always given to runaway slaves.
You will be put on a ship for Rome,
where you will die in the arena before the Emperor,
torn to pieces by wild beasts."

THE VOYAGE TO ROME WAS TERRIBLE.
Androcles and the other prisoners
were loaded with heavy chains
and forced to scrub the decks
and sometimes to row with the galley slaves.

AT LAST THEY REACHED LAND.
The prisoners were taken to the Coliseum,
the huge building where they were to die.
As they waited outside the arena,
they heard the shouts of the excited crowd
and the roars of the wild beasts,
which had been starved for days
to make them hungrier and fiercer.
Androcles was given a thin lance with which to defend himself,
though everyone knew it was useless.
"It's a pity that being hungry doesn't make *me* fiercer.
It only makes me more frightened," Androcles thought.

WHEN IT WAS TIME FOR ANDROCLES TO ENTER THE ARENA,
his legs shook so much that he could hardly stand.
He heard the door clang shut behind him.
Then he heard the wild beasts' cage being opened.
He shut his eyes and waited
to feel the creature's hot breath on his skin
and its sharp teeth meet in his flesh.

But he did not feel any teeth.
No cruel claws tore at his body.
Instead he felt a warm furry head rubbing against his legs
and a rough tongue was licking his feet.
Something was purring like a huge, friendly cat.
He opened his eyes and he saw a lion.
It was a lion he had seen before.
It was a lion he knew well.
It was the lion he had cured
and which had shared his cave in the mountains of Africa.
"It is you! My friend!" Androcles said to the lion,
caressing it, hardly able to believe his good fortune.

"Stop the performance! This is a miracle!"
the Emperor shouted from his box.
"Bring the prisoner here to me."
When Androcles stood before the Emperor
he told the story of his first meeting with the lion.
The Emperor said, "Wonderful!
You shall no longer be a slave, but a free citizen of Rome.
Ask any other favour and if I can I will grant it."
"Sire, my wife, Numia, was taken from me,
with our little son,
to be brought as a slave to Rome.
If I could find her again,
I would ask for nothing more," Androcles said.

NUMIA WAS FOUND AMONG THE EMPEROR'S MANY SLAVES.
She and Androcles were overjoyed to be together again,
with their son, who had grown so much
that Androcles hardly recognised him.
It became one of the famous sights of Rome
to see Androcles walking through the streets
with his friend the lion,
quiet and amiable, by his side.